Dear Parents and Educators,

W9-BOB-604

Welcome to Penguin Young Readers! As parents and educators, you know that each child develops at his or her own pace—in terms of speech, critical thinking, and, of course, reading. Penguin Young Readers recognizes this fact. As a result, each Penguin Young Readers book is assigned a traditional easy-to-read level (1–4) as well as a Guided Reading Level (A–P). Both of these systems will help you choose the right book for your child. Please refer to the back of each book for specific leveling information. Penguin Young Readers features esteemed authors and illustrators, stories about favorite characters, fascinating nonfiction, and more!

Tenkai Knights™
The Power of Four

LEVEL 3

GUIDED READING LEVEL **M**

This book is perfect for a **Transitional Reader** who:
- can read multisyllable and compound words;
- can read words with prefixes and suffixes;
- is able to identify story elements (beginning, middle, end, plot, setting, characters, problem, solution); and
- can understand different points of view.

Here are some **activities** you can do during and after reading this book:
- Vocabulary: Some of the words in this book may be unfamiliar to the child. Find the words below in the text. Look up the definition of the words below in the dictionary, and any other words the child does not understand.

activate	retrieve
assault	taunt
commence	trigger
fortress	ultimate

- Summarize: Work with the child to write a short summary about what happened in the beginning, middle, and end of the story.

Remember, sharing the love of reading with a child is the best gift you can give!

—Bonnie Bader, EdM
 Penguin Young Readers program

*Penguin Young Readers are leveled by independent reviewers applying the standards developed by Irene Fountas and Gay Su Pinnell in *Matching Books to Readers: Using Leveled Books in Guided Reading*, Heinemann, 1999.

PENGUIN YOUNG READERS
Published by the Penguin Group
Penguin Group (USA) LLC, 375 Hudson Street, New York, New York 10014, USA

USA | Canada | UK | Ireland | Australia | New Zealand | India | South Africa | China

penguin.com
A Penguin Random House Company

TM Spin Master Ltd. All rights reserved. © 2014 Spin Master Ltd. / Shogaukuken-Shueisia
Productions Co., Ltd. All rights reserved. Published by Penguin Young Readers, an imprint of
Penguin Group (USA) LLC, 345 Hudson Street, New York, New York 10014. Printed in the USA.

ISBN 978-0-448-48350-4   10 9 8 7 6 5 4 3 2 1

TENKAI KNIGHTS
展開騎士

THE POWER OF FOUR

by Brandon T. Snider

Penguin Young Readers
An Imprint of Penguin Group (USA) LLC

Glossary

Tenkai Knights are warrior robots from the planet **Quarton**.

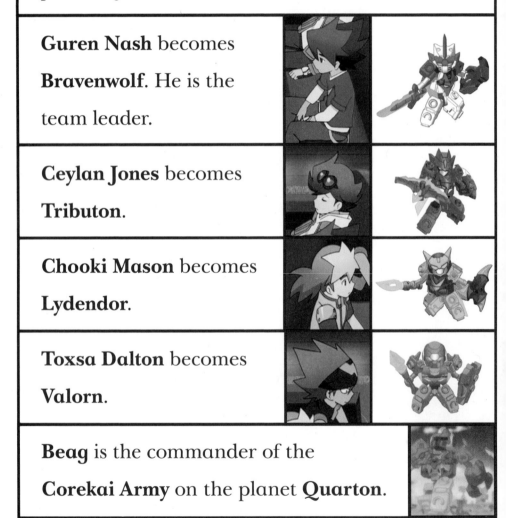

Guren Nash becomes **Bravenwolf**. He is the team leader.

Ceylan Jones becomes **Tributon**.

Chooki Mason becomes **Lydendor**.

Toxsa Dalton becomes **Valorn**.

Beag is the commander of the **Corekai Army** on the planet **Quarton**.

Boreas is one of the four ancient Guardians. He watches over the Interdimensional Portal.

Mr. White owns the **Shop of Wonders**. He is full of secrets.

Vilius was once a Tenkai Knight hero, but he was turned evil by dark forces. He rules an evil army known as **the Corrupted**.

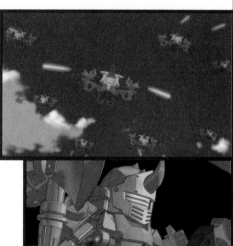

Granox is one of **Vilius**'s favorite soldiers.

Dragon Cubes are pieces of the **Tenkai Dragon**, which was split into five cubes and scattered across the planet **Quarton**.

On the planet **Quarton**, **Tributon** and **Bravenwolf** found one of the **Dragon Cubes**. It was inside a giant fortress. The fortress was guarded by **Granox**, one of **Vilius**'s evil soldiers. **Tributon** and **Bravenwolf** had to be very careful.

"**Tributon**, use your powers!"
shouted **Bravenwolf**. "Shields up,
everyone! We have to get that cube!"

"You **Corekai** are weak. Sky
assault!" said **Granox**, unleashing
an army of Robobeasts.

"**Tributon**, hold your position. **Tenkai Knights** stay together!" said **Bravenwolf**. "We can't lose focus."

Tributon did his best to push back **Granox**'s forces, but the pressure was too much. When the battle became too difficult, he ran away.

"Run away, **Tenkai Knight**! Next time we will find you and destroy you," said **Granox**.

Later, at Mr. White's **Shop of Wonders**, the **Tenkai Knights** met up in their human forms to talk about the battle.

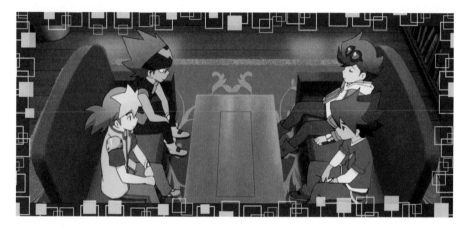

"I wish I could fly," said Chooki. "Then we could have beaten them!"

"Our biggest problem wasn't them, it was *us*," said **Guren**.

Suddenly **Boreas**, one of the four Guardians, appeared with a message for the boys.

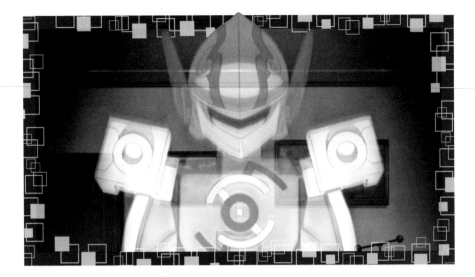

"The **Dragon Cubes** hold the key to ultimate victory. This one must be retrieved immediately. I see the time has finally come for Robofusion!" said **Boreas**. "The four of you must become one."

"You mean there's a way to join our Tenkai Energy with our minds *and* our robot bodies?" asked Chooki. "I guess there's no *I* in *team*."

The boys decided to grab a bite to eat at the diner Toxsa's family ran. They wanted to test their teamwork.

"You boys going to order?" asked Toxsa's sister, Wakame. She was a waitress at the diner.

The boys focused their minds and tried to order the same drink at the same time, but it didn't work. They looked very silly.

"We weren't even close!" said **Guren**. They tried again, but it was no use. They weren't able to think the same thing. How would they be heroes now?

"You won't improve your teamwork sitting around a diner!" said Wakame. She challenged the boys to a soccer game. They could test their skills on the field.

"If you want to be a team, you have to play like a team and get crushed like a team!" Wakame said, laughing. The boys gave it their all during the soccer match, but they still weren't working together. "You don't *think* like a team, you *stink* like a team!" Wakame taunted.

"We have to try harder!" said **Guren**.

Later, Wakame took the boys kayaking. Maybe this would bond them together.

"One mind and one team!" cheered **Guren**.

"Look out!" shouted Wakame as the boys crashed into another kayak. It seemed like they'd never learn how to be a team.

Later that night, **Ceylan**'s dad told him that he had gotten a new job. The family had to move to another city. What would become of the **Tenkai Knights** now?

Ceylan had a lot on his mind.

So he visited the **Shop of Wonders**,

looking for some answers.

"Have the four become one yet?"

asked Mr. White.

"No. They've become three,"
Ceylan said, placing his Tenkai Core
Brick on the table. "I have to give
this back. It's not what I want, but
my family is moving away. I won't be
around anymore."

The rest of the boys soon arrived at the shop.

But before **Ceylan** could share his news, they used the Portal to travel to **Quarton** and changed themselves into the **Tenkai Knights**.

"One mind and one team, here we come! **Tenkai Knights**, GO!" **Guren** shouted.

On **Quarton**, **Bravenwolf** reminded his friends to stay focused. He knew that if they worked together, they could defeat **Granox** once and for all. Each of them trained, and they were finally ready for another shot at victory.

The four **Tenkai Knights** put their heads together, hoping to activate Robofusion. But all they did was bonk one another on the head. "Ouch!" said **Valorn**.

"Ha-ha! Look at these fools! The mighty **Tenkai Knights** are failures. Attack them, my army, and show them true power!" **Granox** shouted as **the Corrupted** moved in to attack.

Granox had unleashed his toughest attack yet. The **Tenkai Knights** lost all their energy and were badly injured. **Tributon** wanted to help his friends. They needed him now more than ever. He couldn't let them down.

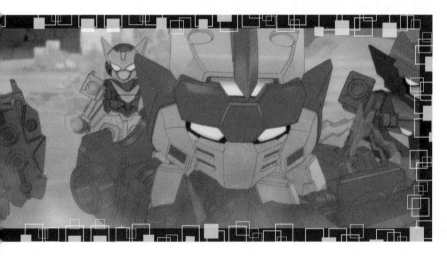

"**Tenkai Knights**, retreat! We still need more practice!" said **Bravenwolf** as the battle raged around him. "Don't worry. We'll get them next time."

"There *is* no next time. I'm moving away next week!" said **Tributon**.

"It's my fault that we can't do that Robofusion thing. I'm sorry. I didn't realize it until now, but you guys are the best friends I've ever had!"

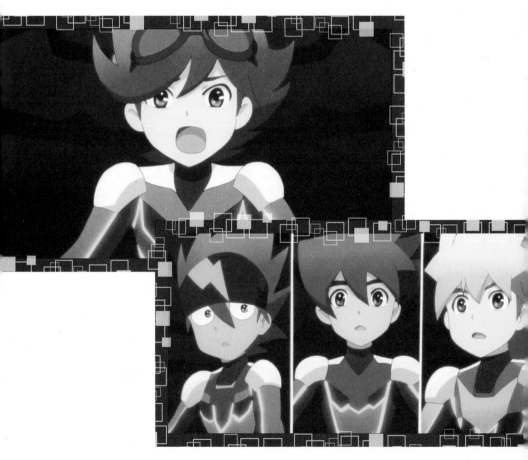

"Tenkai Sync has been achieved! The four have now become one. Commencing Robofusion!" said the AI voice within their armor.

Tributon saying that they were friends was enough to trigger Robofusion. In a flash of light, the four heroes merged together to create a weapon called the Prodojet.

The Prodojet had a secret weapon called the Phoenix Attack. The Prodojet shapeshifted into a flaming bird called a Phoenix that could burn anything that stood in its way.

The Phoenix Attack vaporized **the Corrupted** Army. **Granox** was furious and defeated. "No! It's not possible!" he shouted in anger. "We were so close to victory!" **Vilius** was very disappointed by **Granox**'s failure.

"Victory is ours!" shouted **Beag**.
"The Corrupted have fled, and
we have secured another Dragon
Cube!" Working together, the **Tenkai**
Knights were able to defeat **Granox**
and his army. But what would they
do without **Tributon**?

"No matter where I go, I'll always know that I was once part of an awesome team," **Tributon** said, walking away and leaving his friends forever. The **Tenkai Knights** had won the day, but why did they feel defeated?

The next day at school, **Guren** thought about all the good times he had had with **Ceylan** and how much he was going to miss his jokes. Just as class was about to start, **Guren** felt a tap on his shoulder. **Ceylan** had returned!

"I don't have to move, after all. It was just a false alarm!" said **Ceylan**. "It looks like you're stuck with me, dude. **Tenkai Knights** forever!"